P9-BZB-062

A Gift For

. . . .

From

. . . .

Ready, Set, Pirouette!
Copyright © 2009 Hallmark Licensing, Inc.

Published by Hallmark Books,
a division of Hallmark Cards, Inc.,
Kansas City, MO 64141
Visit us on the Web at www.Hallmark.com.

All rights reserved. No part of this publication may be
reproduced, transmitted, or stored in any form or by any
means without the prior written permission of the publisher.

Editor: Megan Langford
Art Director: Kevin Swanson
Designer: Mary Eakin
Production Artist: Dan Horton
Lettering Artists: Barbara Mizik
and Doug Havach

ISBN: 978-1-59530-218-2
BOK1121
Printed and bound in China
APR11

Hallmark
GIFT BOOKS

Ready, Set, Pirouette!

By **Chelsea Fogleman**
Illustrated by **Maja Andersen**

Sabrina loved *ballet!* She loved her twirly skirt. She loved her pretty pink shoes. She loved learning new moves and their fancy French names. There was only one thing in the world she loved more than ballet.

It was Doug, her pug.

Sabrina took him with her everywhere she went. When she sat down for breakfast, Doug sat down for breakfast. When she rode her bike, Doug ran behind her. When she went to school . . . well, Doug wasn't allowed at school. But he waited all day at the window until she came home.

Doug was especially glad to see Sabrina on Wednesdays. On Wednesdays, Sabrina went to ballet class. And because Mademoiselle said that ballet is for *everyone,* Doug went to ballet class, too.

The class was preparing for their recital—the biggest event of the entire year. The girls couldn't stop talking about it. Some of them even bought new leg warmers just for rehearsals!

This was an especially big year for Sabrina. Mademoiselle
had asked her to do a variation. That meant a solo routine!
And that was a very big deal!

Sabrina practiced every day.

Her battements were *beautiful*.

Her pliés were **perfect**.

And her arabesques were **amazing.**

There was only one problem.

Her pirouettes. That means her turns. Every time she got up on her toes and tried to twirl, she stumbled. Sometimes she got so dizzy she couldn't see straight!

"What am I going to do?" she moaned. "The recital is tomorrow!" Doug trotted over to his doggy bed, grabbed his bone, and dropped it at Sabrina's feet. She laughed. "That's very sweet of you, Doug, but I don't think you can help me this time."

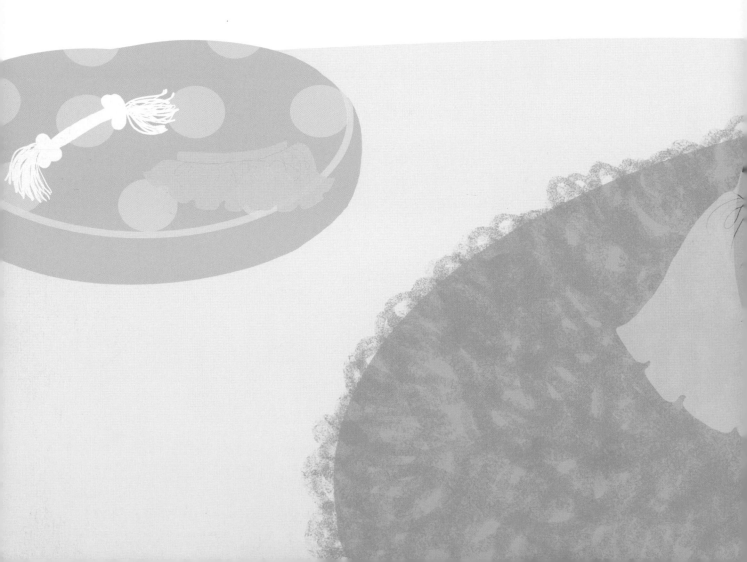

Dance

The next night, Sabrina was ready—well, almost ready. Her hair looked fantastic, her tutu was fluffed just right, and her best friend was there to cheer her on. But she still hadn't quite gotten her pirouettes right.

She paced nervously around backstage. "I don't think I can do this," she said. Doug nuzzled her leg and pushed her toward the stage.

Ready or not, it was showtime.

oooh

Sabrina took a deep breath. When the music started, she glided onto the stage with a smooth glissade. **Oohs** and **ahhs** rose up from the audience.

The performance was going great—until it was time for her first pirouette.

ahh

The instant Sabrina began to twirl, she heard giggles from the crowd. It was just as she had feared.

Then, out of the corner of her eye, she saw a pug . . . chasing his tail. What is Doug doing onstage? Sabrina wondered. But because of Doug, no one even noticed when Sabrina wobbled.

But just a few moments later, it was time for Sabrina's second spin. She felt a wave of anxiety wash over her as she prepared to twirl.

Just as before, Doug appeared onstage. This time, he skipped in on his hind legs. The audience thought the dog was funny! In fact, they couldn't take their eyes off him! And once again, no one seemed to notice Sabrina's not-so-special pirouette.

As she continued dancing, she felt better and better—even as she got ready for the last pesky pirouette! She couldn't turn around to look, but she was sure that Doug was behind her. He knew her routine forward and backward, so he was probably hatching up something really silly to distract the audience for the grand finale.

Here goes, Sabrina told herself. No one will be looking at me, anyway!

Sabrina did a **perfect pirouette!** The crowd burst into applause. Several people stood up. Then more and more people got to their feet. It was incredible!

Sabrina peeked behind her, sure that she'd find Doug trotting offstage—but he was nowhere to be seen.

He didn't come onstage this time, Sabrina realized—
and I did it! That means that they're clapping for . . . *me!*

Sabrina did a perfect little révérence (that means she
curtsied) and skipped offstage.

Doug practically knocked Sabrina over as he showered her with doggy kisses.

"You knew I could do it, didn't you?" she cried, ruffling his ears.

"Woof!" barked Doug.

That meant *yes.*

If you enjoyed this book,
we'd love to hear from you!

Please send your comments to:
Hallmark Book Feedback
P.O. Box 419034
Mail Drop 215
Kansas City, MO 64141

Or e-mail us at:
booknotes@hallmark.com

Dégagé

Pirouette

Freestyle

Battement

Glissade